ONE UNICORN

written and illustrated by Gale Cooper

A Unicorn Book · E. P. Dutton · New York

LIBRARY OF CONGRESS CATALOGING IN PUBLICATION DATA

Cooper, Gale.   One unicorn.
(A Unicorn book)

Summary: A unicorn repeatedly appears to Princess
Alicia until she loses her childhood innocence.
[1. Unicorns—Fiction]   I. Title.
PZ7.C7852On   1981   [Fic]   81-4037
ISBN 0-525-36438-2   AACR2

Published in the United States by Elsevier-Dutton
Publishing Co., Inc., 2 Park Avenue, New York, N.Y. 10016

Published simultaneously in Canada by Clarke,
Irwin & Company Limited, Toronto and Vancouver

Editor: Emilie McLeod   Designer: Claire Counihan

Printed in the U.S.A.   First Edition
10 9 8 7 6 5 4 3 2 1

for Rudy Vaca, Zvi Sella,
Thea Sella and Emil Sella

with special thanks
to Alan Murray, Emilie McLeod, Sid Fleischman,
Nanette Gorgone, Shannon Toon, Albert Ostermaier,
John Theobald, Don Thompson, Susan Temple,
Lisa Lenz, Ron Keith, and Linda Keith

Centuries ago when unicorns roamed the earth, there lived, in a mighty castle of stone, a kind and just king and his fair young daughter, the princess Alicia. She was his sole heir and only reminder of his beautiful queen, whose life ended soon after Alicia's birth.

In his sorrow, the king decreed that no pain, sadness, loneliness, doubt, or boredom should ever mar Alicia's life. She was to have all manner of maids, toys, pets, teachers, musicians, and magicians. Everything she saw must be beautiful. Everything she touched must be soft and gentle. The finest fragrances and the most joyful music filled the air of her chambers. Everyone smiled or laughed in her presence. Princess Alicia was indeed content.

And on the fiftieth day of the fiftieth year of his prosper-ous reign, when the land was blooming with spring, the king left Alicia and went, as each generation of his ancestors had done, to claim his birthright—the prophecy of what was to come after him. The future would be revealed to him as a reward for goodness done and as a lesson for errors made.

Early in the morning on this special day, the king walked into the deep, green forest. Accompanied only by his favorite dogs, he followed a narrow, overgrown path taught to him in childhood by his parents. The path ended in a distant clearing filled with music more beautiful than any he had ever heard.

Spirit creatures waited there as they had waited on the fiftieth day of the fiftieth year of his father's reign. From the time of golden sunlight to the time of purple starlight, he was whirled and turned in a magic dance. Abruptly the music ceased, the dancing stopped, and an ancient spirit stepped forward. She sang,

> Mother of Darkness
> Father of Light
> Give this King
> His birthgiven Right.

Then she spoke the prophecy. "The rewards for generosity and honesty are health, prosperity, and peace. Death will come as a welcome friend, for there is time to complete your earthly tasks.

"You have made only one error, kind King. In your great love for Princess Alicia, you have protected her from all pain. She is a prisoner of innocence and knows nothing of the world. You have no right to control another's fate, or to prevent the pain of living. Therefore, it will come to pass that though she too will have health, prosperity, and long life, her heart will be broken at a tender age. In the midst of happiness there will always be a reminder of pain. Man cannot know the deepest secret of the balance of all things, but be satisfied in knowing that this pain will make her wise. She will be a queen well loved and long remembered."

Saddened, the king watched the spirits resume their dance and fade into a rainbow of whirling mist. At midnight, nothing remained of them but dewdrops glistening in the moonlight. The king retraced the secret path to the castle where he slept a deep, long sleep.

In the early morning of the fifty-first day of the fiftieth year of her father's reign, Princess Alicia awoke with a strange longing left from a forgotten dream. Without calling her old nurse, or even tying back her long, golden hair, she hurried into the misty green forest.

Alicia was only mildly surprised that her feet led her through a winding narrow path to a clearing deep in the forest. There grew one exquisite and fragrant milk white flower. Its center was of the brightest gold. She knelt beside it and saw herself reflected in the dewdrops jeweling its leaves and petals. Since anything of beauty that she had ever wanted had been given to her, she reached to pick the flower. Knowing nothing of thorns, she was most surprised and somewhat angered by a needle-sharp pain as she grasped the stem.

A drop of blood stained her finger, and she cried for the first time in her life. One great tear rolled down her cheek and dropped into one diamond bright dewdrop on the flower.

The tiny puddle began to grow. In its center she saw a cloudy form. Forgetting both tears and pain, she watched a miniature creature take shape. Bigger and bigger it grew until the flower itself became a glistening sac. Within it lay sleeping a perfectly formed white creature with golden hooves and a golden spiraling horn. It stirred and the horn pierced the delicate covering. The animal struggled to unsteady legs, shook the water from its snowy coat, and stared at the princess with huge blue eyes.

"You must be a unicorn," she said delightedly, and took him in her arms. With contentment he nestled in her lap. Alicia held the sleeping unicorn until it was late afternoon and she had to return to the castle.

There she asked questions about the great tapestries picturing unicorn hunts. Fear widened her eyes when the huntsmen spoke greedily of the double weight in gold to be paid for a horn, hoof, bone, or pelt of one unicorn. A man could drink fearlessly from a cup made of unicorn horn because it made harmless any poison. When powdered and mixed in a potion of wine, the horn cured every human illness. A cloak or even a belt of the skin made a man invisible and invincible in battle. One smooth round ankle-bone worn as an amulet made faint men strong and strong men irresistible in love. But all huntsmen believed that the unicorn was a savage untamable beast, too powerful to be captured easily. Tales were told of many who had been run through by the cruel horn and devoured piece by piece.

All that springtime the unicorn grew rapidly. During morning study, afternoon nap, or even after bedtime, the princess secretly slipped away to visit him. They would meet deep in the forest, hidden from the huntsmen's bloodthirsty swords. She rode on his strong back, his shimmering mane and her blonde tresses tangling in the wind.

On the last day of spring, the unicorn said, "My dearest Princess, you must remember that a unicorn can exist only when nourished by pure love. The violence men see in our kind is a mirror of their own cruelty. My death will come only when your innocence is lost."

> Sadness, sadness, heartfelt pain
> If all the love has been in vain.
> If you ever speak a lie,
> Then, my friend, I will die.

Laughing, Princess Alicia pressed his head to her bosom. "Then you will live forever, for why should I ever lie to you, dear unicorn?" And it seemed he would, for all the days of that magic summer were woven through with rainbows, sunlight, moonlight, and shooting stars.

On the first day of autumn the king called his daughter to him and said, "The warmth of your beauty has spared me the chill of old age. Now the time comes for you to marry. I have made arrangements for you to meet Prince Nicholas. He is of a rich and noble family. He is said to be wise and kind."

The princess was silent. She thought only of the unicorn and had no interest in the prince.

Autumn leaves fell and winter frost rode on the winds. Then a great caravan came to the castle, bringing rich gifts from Prince Nicholas to honor the princess. She took the jewels and golden ribbons, and braided them in the unicorn's mane, and thought not at all of the prince.

When the first frost of winter silvered the land, black-haired Prince Nicholas arrived on a stallion as red as blood. The prince's dark eyes filled with joy when he beheld the beauty of Princess Alicia. Her heart opened, for never had she seen a man more fair. Many a day passed with her gazing into the darkness of his eyes while he marveled at the blueness of hers. She forgot the unicorn.

When at last Alicia went to the forest, the unicorn said, "I have missed you, my Princess."

"I forgot our meetings, dear unicorn. Many have been my joys, and the days have slipped away."

"You speak truthfully," he said, "but the cold of winter chills my heart."

> Sadness, sadness, heartfelt pain
> If all the love has been in vain.
> If you ever speak a lie,
> Then, my friend, I will die.

Together they galloped through the first flakes of snow and they were happy.

Snow in great drifts soon covered the land. The princess sat by the fireside while Prince Nicholas told tales of savage dragons and brave heroes. She remembered the unicorn, but she chose to remain beside the warmth of the fire and with the prince.

It was not until the melting snow began to feed small streams with its water, that the princess returned to the forest. The unicorn's eyes were filled with sadness. "Many weeks have passed," he said.

"I forgot our meetings, as before," she lied and cast down her eyes.

"You do not speak the truth. The time of your innocence is over," he said softly. They raced in the melting snow, but when the princess dismounted, the unicorn followed her to the forest's edge. There he stood in full view of the huntsmen, his white coat vivid against the black soaked earth.

Princess Alicia turned at the baying call of the hounds. She saw the spear and arrow flying to their mark. The unicorn shuddered and fell. Never did his eyes leave her. She ran to him and pulled his head onto her lap. Blood stained his whiteness and silently her tears fell.

The unicorn murmured, "Your lie is forgiven, my Princess."

> Sadness, sadness, heartfelt pain
> If all the love has been in vain.
> When you spoke the single lie,
> That marked, dear friend, my time to die.

The huntsmen stood waiting to claim their prize. Suddenly about them swirled a rainbow mist. Quickly it cleared and nothing remained but a glistening of dewdrops on the lap of the princess and the ground beside her.

On the first day of the new spring, the princess and Prince Nicholas were married. As the bridal procession passed the edge of the forest, Alicia saw, in the very place where the unicorn had disappeared, a bush filled with glorious blossoms, some as red as blood, some as white as snow. The princess stopped and plucked one blossom of each color and joined them to her wedding bouquet.

One year later, the old king died and Alicia became queen. She ordered that the bush of red and white blossoms be taken from the edge of the forest and planted in the castle courtyard. Soon a daughter was born to Queen Alicia and King Nicholas. The child grew more beautiful with every happy day.

But sometimes the wind blew memories along with the perfume of the blossoms, and the good queen secretly watered the flowering bush with her tears. She sang a mournful song,

> Sadness, sadness, heartfelt pain
> If all the love has been in vain.
> If again I speak a lie,
> Then, my friend, I will die.

One such night in spring, the young princess heard her words, and she dreamed of a milk white creature with golden hooves and one spiraling horn.

When the child told her of the dream, Queen Alicia smiled. She realized that for each person whose heart is filled with innocence and love, there can be one unicorn.